T3-BWP-636

BEAR'S
BRIGHT IDEA

Written by Meredith Costain
Illustrated by Kate Curtis

Max and Bear are playing a fast game of soccer.

Look at Bear's tongue!

Running around is hard work.

Look how red Max's face and arms are getting.

He's getting too hot to keep playing.

Now Max is starting to sweat.

A cold drink will help cool Max down.

And it's much cooler in the shade.

Oh-oh. A chilly breeze whips around the garden.

Look at those goosebumps on Max's arms.

Brrr! Max is starting to shiver.

What can he do to warm up again?

Max could play another game with Bear.

Putting his jacket back on would help too.

Bear knows what to do!

Look! He's found them a nice warm spot in the sun.

Parent and Teacher Notes

The story of Bear's Bright Idea looks at the science of heat:

Our bodies like their core temperature to be not too hot and not too cold, but just right – at around 37°C.

EXPERIMENT
Make Your Own Thermometer

What you need:
- a glass bottle
- cold water
- food colouring
- a large clear plastic drinking straw
- plasticine/modelling clay
- coloured marker pens.

What you do:
1. Add cold water to the bottle until it is about three-quarters full.
2. Add a couple of drops of food colouring to the water.
3. Put the straw into the bottle. Don't let it touch the bottom.
4. Seal around the straw with plasticine/modelling clay. Make sure it's air-tight!
5. Blow into the straw until water rises half-way up it. Put a black mark on the bottle to show the water level when the temperature is normal.
6. Put the bottle in a warm place for an hour. Mark the new water level in red.
7. Put the bottle in the fridge for an hour. Mark the new water level in blue.

Which temperature made the water level rise? Which temperature made the water level fall?

How Does Our Body Temperature Stay Just Right?

When we get too hot, our bodies work hard to release the extra heat. Blood vessels just under our skin carry extra blood to the surface, making our skin look red, and sweat appears on the surface of the skin to cool us down.

When we're too cold, our bodies try to keep the heat in. 'Goosebumps' form on our skin when muscles contract to make our hairs stand on end to trap heat. Our muscles move up and down, producing heat as they make us shiver.

We can help our bodies maintain an even temperature by adding or removing clothes, drinking hot or cool drinks, or moving to a warm or shady spot, in or out of the sun.

What about dogs' temperatures? When dogs are hot they don't sweat, they pant. Panting helps them lose heat from their bodies. When dogs are cold, their thick fur stands on end, trapping a layer of warm air close to their bodies to help keep them nice and warm.

About the Author

Meredith Costain is a versatile, award-winning author who specialises in books for early childhood. Many of her titles have sold internationally or been adapted for television, audio or multi-media. She lives in inner-city Melbourne with a menagerie of pets, who frequently feature in her stories.

About the Illustrator

Kate Curtis has had fun drawing pictures in advertising, animation and comics for a very long time, and counts dogs among her closest friends. She divides her time between a very old house in inner-city Melbourne and a very old house at Point Lonsdale.

The Five Mile Press Pty Ltd
1 Centre Road, Scoresby
Victoria 3179 Australia
www.fivemile.com.au

Written by Meredith Costain

Science at Play series copyright © The Five Mile Press, 2009
Text copyright © The Five Mile Press, 2009
Illustrations copyright © Kate Curtis, 2009
All rights reserved
Series editor: Niki Horin

First published 2009

Printed in China 5 4 3 2 1

National Library of Australia Cataloguing-in-Publication data
          Costain, Meredith, 1955-
          Bear's bright idea / Meredith Costain ; illustrator, Kate Curtis.
          9781742115023 (hbk.)
          Costain, Meredith, 1955-   Science at play
          For primary school age.
          Heat--Juvenile literature
          Curtis, Kate